In loving memory of Marguerite Davol
JK

To Ilana,
for your part in who I am
GB

First edition 2022

Library of Congress Catalog Card Number pending
ISBN 978-1-5362-0783-5

21 22 23 24 25 26 CCP 10 9 8 7 6 5 4 3 2 1

Printed in Shenzhen, Guangdong, China

This book was typeset in Badger.
The illustrations were created digitally.

Candlewick Press
99 Dover Street
Somerville, Massachusetts 02144

www.candlewick.com

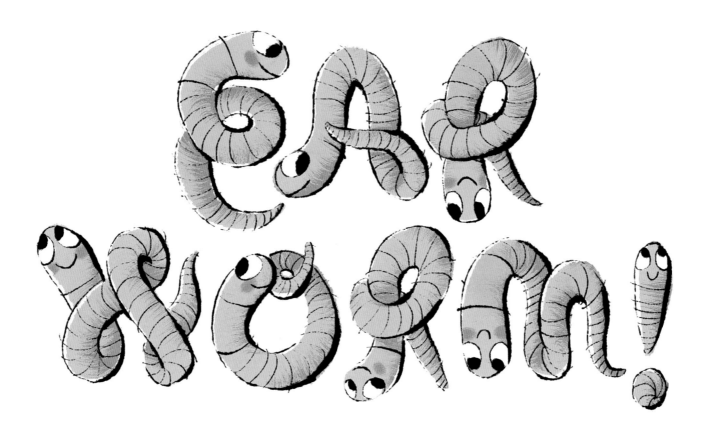

# EAR WORM!

**Jo Knowles**        illustrated by **Galia Bernstein**

CANDLEWICK PRESS

One summer day, Little Worm went out to play and discovered he had a song stuck in his head.

"Shimmy shimmy, no-sashay,

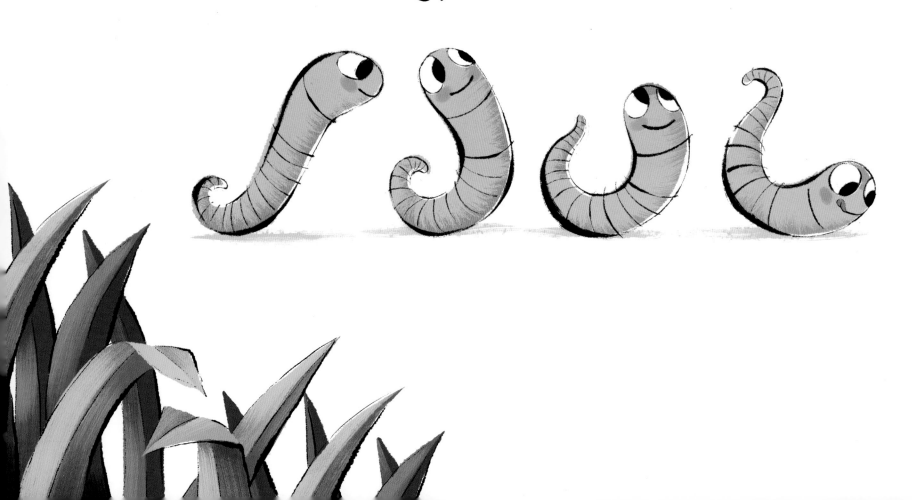

shimmy shimmy, no-sashay!"

he sang as he wriggled along.

Owl stopped to say hello.

"Good morning, Little Worm," he said. "What's that you're singing?"

"I don't know," said Little Worm, "but I can't get it out of my head!"

"You have an ear worm!" said Owl.

"A what?" asked Little Worm.

"An ear worm is what happens when a song gets stuck in your head."

"That's a funny name," said Little Worm.

he sang again, swaying this way and that.

"Did you put this song in my head?" asked Little Worm.

"It wasn't me," said Owl. "My song goes like this:

WAVE, WAVE, WAVE, TALK TO THE WING! WAAAAVE, WAVE, WAVE, TALK to THE WING!"

He flapped one wing, then the other, dancing to and fro.

"That's a nice one," said Little Worm.
"But I want to find out who put
this song in my head."

"Mind if I come along?"
asked Owl.

"Be my guest!"
said Little Worm.
So:

"WAAAAAAVE, WAAAAAAAVE, TALK to THE WING!"

and

"Shimmy shimmy, no-sashay!"

they went along.

Chipmunk chittered at Little Worm.

"What are you two singing?"

"The songs that are stuck in our heads," said Little Worm.

"You have ear worms!" declared Chipmunk.

Little Worm nodded. "But I don't know where mine came from! Did you put it there?"

"It wasn't me," said Chipmunk. "My song goes like this:

CHEE CHEE, CHITTER-EE!

PUFF YOUR CHEEKS AND DANCE Like ME!"

Chipmunk did a perfect
box step, then ate a nut.

"That's not it at all," said Little Worm. "But I like your moves!"

"Thank you," said Chipmunk. "Mind if I join your search?"

"Fine by me," said Little Worm.

So:

"CHEE CHEE, CHITTER-EE!"

"WAVE, WAVE,

TALK to THE *WING!*"

and

"Shimmy shimmy, no-sashay!"

they went along.

Bunny hopped into the path with a quiet landing.
"What's all this racket?" she asked.
"I'm trying to find out who put this song in my head,"
said Little Worm.
"Everyone gets ear worms," said Bunny. She wiggled
her ears as if she could shake out a song.

"Did you give it
to me?" asked
Little Worm.

"Nope," said Bunny.
"My song goes like this:

Hip-Hop, THUMP-JUMP! Hip-Hop, thump-JUMP!"

"You sure have style," said Little Worm. "Oh, I'll never find out who put this song in my head!"

"Maybe I can help," said Bunny.
So:

"Shimmy Shimmy, No-Sashay!"

Little Worm started to sing, but his heart wasn't in it.

"WAAAAAAVE, WAAAAAAVE, TALK to THE WING!"

Owl sang and danced to cheer him up.

"CHEE CHEE, CHITTER-EE!"

Chipmunk joined in.

"HiP-HOP, THUMP-JUMP!"

Bunny put extra pizzazz into her bounce.

"What's going on here?"
asked Fox as she trotted up
the path.

"We have songs stuck in our heads," said Little Worm.
"You have ear worms!" declared Fox.
Little Worm nodded. "Did you put them there?"

"No, my song goes like this!" said Fox.
Fox danced in a dainty circle.

"Rah-Rah, TROT TO ME! RAH-RAH, TROT TROT, to ME!"

Soon everyone was dancing and singing!

Little Worm was
having so much fun,
he forgot all about
trying to find out
who put the song
in his head.

"Little Worm! Little Worm!" called a voice. "It's time for your nap! Come on back home!"
"I guess I'll never know who put this song in my head," Little Worm said as he shimmied home to his papa.

Papa Worm tucked Little Worm into bed.

Then Papa Worm returned to his chores, singing as he went:

"Shimmy shimmy, no-sashay. TIME to NAP, THEN TIME to PLAY. Dance ALONG AND Sing ALL DAY, shimmy shimmy, no-sashay!"

Little Worm opened one eye.
"Ohhhhhh," he said.

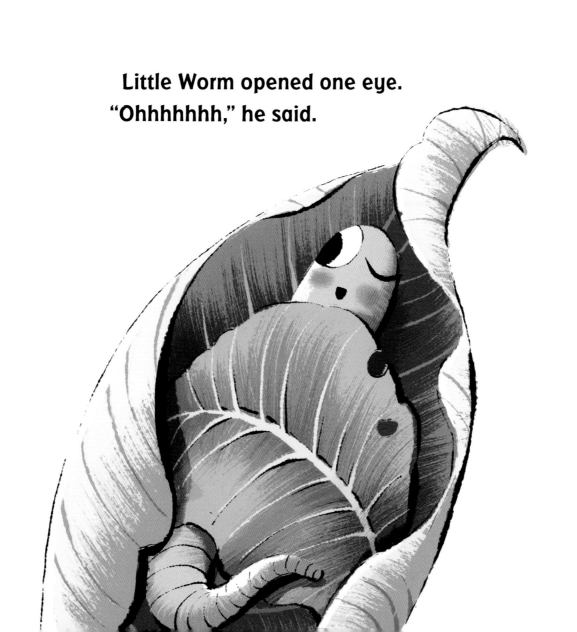

Then he quietly sang along, until he fell fast asleep.

"Shimmy shimmy, no sashay!"